A VISIT TO THE
MONASTERY

PAMELA PAUL HUTCHINGS
Illustrated by Marian Adams

XULON PRESS

Xulon Press
2301 Lucien Way #415
Maitland, FL 32751
407.339.4217
www.xulonpress.com

© 2021 by Pamela Paul Hutchings

Paperback ISBN-13: 978-1-6628-1730-4
Hardcover ISBN-13: 978-1-6628-1731-1
eBook ISBN-13: 978-1-6628-1732-8

Acknowledgements:

I am so thankful to God for giving me the courage, guidance and enthusiasm to write this book. Without question, I had divine direction in finding a most talented artist, Marian Adams! Her watercolors and her personal devotion to the project are so appreciated. I am also grateful to the amazing monastic communities which gave me inspiration for this book: Sacred Monastery of St. Nina, Union Bridge, Maryland; St. Barbara Monastery, Santa Paula, California; Holy Assumption Monastery, Calistoga, California; The Holy Monastery of the Theotokos the Life Giving Spring, Dunlap, California; and The Annunciation of the Theotokos Monastery, Reddick, Florida. My exceptional visits with the Sisters and their intercessory prayers have been a great blessing. I also thank Fr. Jacques Jude LePine and Abbess Victoria of St. Barbara Monastery for their scholarly Orthodox assistance. A very special thank you to my friend, Lisa St. Clair, for her editorial and translation services. A sincere, heartfelt thanks to my husband, Don, and our children, Julie, Jay and Brady for their love and encouragement.

Pamela

For James, whose encouragement and love is behind every brushstroke, and for my parents, who raised me in the Faith and took me to visit monasteries.

All my love,
M

This Book Belongs to

<u>Calvin</u>   <u>from</u>   <u>Grammy Jo</u>

I Love you!   2022

Today we will visit the monastery
to celebrate the
Feast Day of Saint Anna.

Everywhere we see fields of
lavender and sunflowers.

The beautiful countryside is
God's glorious creation.

The monastery is a holy place.

Here the nuns live together.
They welcome all the visitors.

Sister Katherine
rings the Church bells.
"Come and see", she says.

We make the sign of the Cross and enter into the Church. We light candles, pray and sing.

The Priest shares the story of Saint Anna,
the mother of the Holy Virgin Mary.
At the altar, we receive Holy Communion.

The Priest leads everyone in a procession around the Church.

He holds a beautiful icon
honoring Saint Anna.

After Church, the mothers
help the nuns in
the kitchen.

A Feast Day meal
is prepared
and the Priest gives
the blessing.
Everyone enjoys the feast!

Later the men
and the boys help
with the chores.

Sister Olga shows us
where their chickens live.
We collect the eggs.

Here is their vegetable garden.

Sister Nectaria shows us
the honeybee hives.
The nuns collect the
honey to sell.

Sister
Thekla opens
the dovecote.

She says
that we should always
"be gentle as doves".

There is a tire swing
by the stream.

Friendly peacocks
with radiant colors
remind us that
God made all
the creatures
on earth.

21

We love story time with Sister Marina.
She tells us that God wants us
to guard our hearts...

...and that we can
make our hearts
like a monastery.
She gives a prayer rope
to each child.

She teaches us how to pray
"The Prayer of the Heart".

Sister Helena paints holy icons of Saints in her studio.

24

The Saints are
like family members.
The Saints are
heroes of
our Faith.

25

The nuns collect lavender
from the fields and
make sachets to sell
at festivals.

Time for tea and cookies.
A monastery cat lives here, too.

At dusk, we go inside the Church.

The nuns pray for us and
for all the people in the world.

29

As we prepare to leave, we thank the nuns for this special day. We understand why they chose to live a holy life here.

We are thankful to God for all of
His blessings and for our friends,
the nuns at the monastery.

We can live a holy life, too.

These verses from Holy Scripture can help us to guard our hearts.

In everything, give thanks. (1 Thessalonians 5:18)

The Lord loves holy hearts. (Proverbs 22:12)

God is love. (1 John 4:8)

God loves a cheerful giver. (2 Corinthians 9:7)

God lives in me. (1 Corinthians 3:16)

Blessed are the pure in heart for they shall see God. (Matthew 5:8)

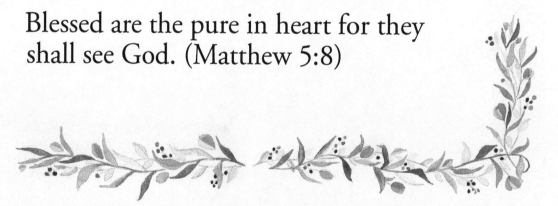

The Prayer of the Heart

"Lord Jesus Christ, Son of God,
have mercy on me."

"Lord, help me to
make my heart like
a monastery."
(From Saint Luke, the surgeon)

9 781662 817304